THE CREEPER DIARIES

BOOK THREE

NEW CREEP AT SCHOOL

THE CREEPER DIARIES

BOOK THREE

NEW CREEP AT SCHOOL

GREYSON MANN
ILLUSTRATED BY AMANDA BRACK

Sky Pony Press
New York

Copyright © 2017 by Hollan Publishing, Inc.

Minecraft® is a registered trademark of Notch Development AB.

The Minecraft game is copyright © Mojang AB.

Sky Pony Press books may be purchased in bulk at special discounts for sales promotion, corporate gifts, fund-raising, or educational purposes. Special editions can also be created to specifications. For details, contact the Special Sales Department, Sky Pony Press, 307 West 36th Street, 11th Floor, New York, NY 10018 or info@skyhorsepublishing.com.

Sky Pony® is a registered trademark of Skyhorse Publishing, Inc.®, a Delaware corporation.

Visit our website at www.skyponypress.com.

10 9 8 7 6 5 4 3 2 1

Library of Congress Cataloging-in-Publication Data is available on file.

Special thanks to Erin L. Falligant.

Cover illustration by Amanda Brack
Cover design by Brian Peterson

Hardcover ISBN: 978-1-5107-3112-7
E-book ISBN: 978-1-5107-3113-4

Printed in the United States of America

DAY 1: THURSDAY

So last night was pretty much the best school night EVER.

See, we got this new creep at school. And by "creep," I do mean creeper. As in, another creeper like me. At Mob Middle School. In sixth grade. FINALLY. Let me tell you, I've been waiting for this moment for like my whole life—or at LEAST all semester.

I haven't had a creeper to hang out with since my friend Cash moved away. We both loved making up rap songs and setting off fireworks.

Since then, the only friends I've had are a bouncy slime and a flesh-eating zombie. And Ziggy Zombie is pretty far down my "Top Two Friends" checklist, believe me.

Top Two Friends

1. Sam Slime

$1\frac{1}{4}$.

$1\frac{1}{2}$.

$1\frac{3}{4}$.

2. Ziggy Zombie

Sam is alright, but he's no Cash Creeper. I mean, Sam would NEVER fling a mushroom at a cat. He's got this black and white cat named Moo, and he's always going on and on about her. He got this Cat Cam for his birthday, and now he takes videos of Moo. Which means that I have to WATCH the videos. Over and over again. Even though I've made it perfectly clear that I don't like cats.

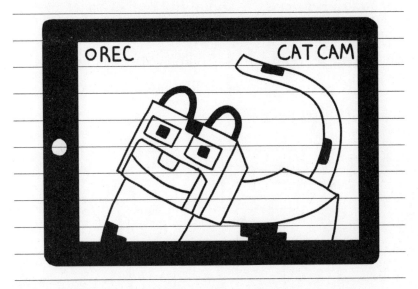

If I see ONE more video of Moo falling off the bookshelf or squeezing into a flowerpot or batting at her carrot on a stick, I'm going to barf all over Sam's Cat Cam.

He's always like, "No, wait! You have to see this next one!" And pretty soon I'm watching Sam and Moo share mushroom stew. One spoonful for her (lick, lick, lick), and one spoonful for him. GROSS. Sometimes I think there's something seriously wrong with that slime.

So when Connor Creeper walked into my first period Language Arts class, I about fell out of my chair. I knew he was cool from the moment I laid eyes on the dude. So did Mrs. Collins, our teacher. She probably agrees that we could use a few more creepers around here.

After she introduced him to the class, she asked him to take a seat between me and Chloe, my Evil Twin. "Chloe can tell you about some of the extracurriculars we offer here at Mob Middle School," she said. "Blah, blah, blah."

Chloe sat straight up—she seemed pretty excited about that. See, she's all about Strategic Exploding class after school, because she's always looking for another reason to blow up. But me? Not so much. I use my brains instead of my blasts. And the last thing Connor Creeper needs is to fall in with my twin and the other Strategic Exploders that run around this school with their fuses half-lit.

Turns out, I didn't have to worry about it. Connor said, "Thank you, Mrs. Collins, but I prefer to focus on my studies after school." He flashed her one of those polite smiles that teachers eat right up. And I saw Chloe kind of wilt in her desk. So maybe Connor is more of a brains guy like me.

As he was walking toward the empty seat, I saw Bones gearing up to give him grief. Bones and his skeleton buddies have made my life miserable from day one here at Mob Middle School. So I guess Bones thought he was going to do it all over again with Connor.

I tried to catch Connor's eye to warn him. But I was too late. Right when he walked by that skeleton, Bones started mocking him. "I PREFER to focus on my studies after school, Mrs. Collins," he said in a high, whiny whisper. But Bones dropped his pencil while he was doing it. And I watched Connor step RIGHT on that pencil and break it. On purpose. He kind of smiled while he was doing it, too.

So I don't think I have to teach Connor much about Mob Middle School after all. He's already got all the important stuff down.

And I haven't even told you what happened at lunch when I ran into Connor. Well, I didn't really RUN into him. I was sort of stalking him. When I saw him heading toward the vending machine, I walked right by whistling. It didn't work the first time, so I walked by again.

Well that worked great, because he looked up and offered me a pork chop. He plunked an emerald into the vending machine, and when the chop popped out, he tossed it to me—just like that. I told him I'd pay him back, but he said not to worry about it. And when Sam bounced over to say hello, Connor bought HIM a pork chop, too. It was like the dude had this endless supply of emeralds or something.

When we all sat down to eat, I was pretty pumped up to have Connor sitting at our table. Everyone stared at us, kind of like when my buddy Eddy Enderman teleports over to say hello. It doesn't happen very often, but we're SORT of friends. And whenever he talks to me, everyone stares.

So, yeah, everyone was staring at Connor. I was too. Because . . . did I mention he's a creeper?

Then Ziggy Zombie staggered over and just about wrecked the moment. He sat down with a groan and unwrapped his rotten-flesh sandwich. He was so into that stinky sandwich that he didn't even notice Connor was sitting with us. And when Ziggy started eating, Connor said everything I have ALWAYS wanted to say to Ziggy. Every. Single. Word.

He was like, "Dude, can you close your mouth when you eat?" and "Wow, that is one SMELLY sandwich" and "Are you about DONE now?"

Ziggy didn't take the hint.

But he finally noticed Connor. He did a double-take, looking from me to Connor and back again like he thought Connor was my twin or something. Well, THAT was kind of cool. I'd gladly trade Chloe for this guy.

So pretty soon, I was making a plan in my head. A plan for how to turn my SOON-to-be new best friend into my REAL new best friend. And I couldn't wait to get home in the morning after school to write it all down.

See, I'm kind of a goal guy. I like to make a plan and write it down in my journal. If I don't, I'm afraid I'm going to wake up one day and be old and depressed, wondering where my life went. Like my teenage sister, Cate. But that's another story.

I think I got the planning thing from my mom. She's always on some kick, like her "30 Days to a Greener You" diet. Or the month she spent getting into shape with her Zombie Zumba DVDs.

I kind of miss those days, because her latest kick is really getting me down—and making me itch. Mom's sister Constance, who lives up in the hills, sent her this book called *Knit Your Way to Happiness*. And ever since then, she's been tangled up in a ginormous ball of yarn.

I can hear the knitting needles clacking in there, and every once in a while, her head pops out and she tosses me or my sisters a pair of mismatched socks. Or a stocking cap with a big pom-pom on the end. Or one of those "infinity scarves" that never ends. Or, WORST of all, an itchy sweater.

This morning when I got home from school, she met me at the door with a blanket. When I saw Dad sitting on the sofa in an ugly, lumpy sweater, I thought I'd gotten off easy. "Thanks, Mom!" I said. "I'll go put it on my bed right now."

But it turned out it WASN'T a blanket. Mom showed me the hole in the middle and said I was supposed to stick my head through it. And actually WEAR it.

"It's a poncho!" she said, all proud-like.

A WHAT now?

I couldn't believe Mom would actually make me something like that ON PURPOSE. It looked more like my sister Cammy, the Exploding Baby, had blown a hole through a blanket, and Mom was just making the best of it.

Either way, I wasn't wearing that thing. EVER. I mean, except for when Mom made me put it on so she could take a picture to send to Constance.

Then I pulled it back off right away and escaped to my room, where I itched my skin raw. I mean, I have itchy skin anyway. Mom KNOWS this! But, whatever.

Let her knit her way to happiness. I have my own kind of plan, and it has SQUAT to do with ponchos.

I figure I have 30 days to buddy up to Connor. If I don't do it right away, some other mob is going to rattle, stagger, or slime their way in, and then he'll be like, "Gerald? Gerald who?" That's how things work in sixth grade, I'm telling you. I gotta act fast.

So here's my plan:

30 Days to a New Best Friend

- Show Connor how awesome I am (easy, right?)
- Stick close to Connor at school (so he can SEE my awesomeness every second of every school night)
- Give Sam some lessons in playing it cool (so the slime doesn't blow it for me)

I'll get going on that first part right away. Showing Connor how awesome I am WILL be easy. Because I have a super-secret skill that most creepers don't have.

I can RAP.

I write lyrics all the time in my head. Like right now, I'm writing some about Bones. I don't even have to try. All I have to do is write them down so I can practice before school tonight and show Connor my skills. It goes like this:

Listen up, Bones
Sitting on your throne,
You're going down
with a grunt and groan.

Listen up, yo
Watch your bony back,
You're going down - whatcha
think about that?

16

Yup. With Connor Creeper on my side, Bones's days as Mob Middle School's number-one bully are numbered. Creepers are rising up. Skeletons are going down.

DAY 2: FRIDAY

So I'm not going to panic yet, but I MIGHT have to rethink my plan. Turns out, Connor doesn't like rap. HUH. Who knew?

Last night at school, I had it all worked out. I walked by his locker doing my thing.

Listen up, Bones,
Sitting on your throne,
You're going down
With a grunt and groan.

I had to whisper when some of Bones's skeleton buddies rattled on by. But as soon as they were gone, I picked it right up again.

18

I even pretended to get a drink of water at the fountain by Connor's locker, just so he could hear the second verse. And he heard me alright. He was like, "What's up with the rap, creep?"

I THOUGHT it was my big moment. I shrugged all cool-like and told him I was going to be a famous rapper someday, like Kid Z. But you know what he said?

Say WHAT??? It was like my Evil Twin had just strategically exploded, knocking me off my feet. But you know what came out of my mouth next? I told Connor that I wasn't really into Kid Z either.

I actually SAID that—even though Kid Z is my idol. Even though I have posters of him all over my bedroom walls. Even though if I could meet only ONE famous person in the WHOLE Overworld, it'd be him.

So what was I SAYING???

Sam bounced over right about then and asked the question out loud.

What are you saying, Gerald? You LOVE Kid Z!

Well, I mean I wouldn't use the word LOVE. No, I'd probably go with something like "I LOOK UP to Kid Z." But standing there staring at Connor Creeper,

I couldn't come up with any words at all. I felt like someone had stolen them all right out of my mouth.

So instead, I turned on Sam. I'm not proud of it, but I mean, he DID almost blow my big chance with Connor.

I said, "No I don't, Sam. You're the one who LOVES Kid Z. Like you LOVE Willow Witch. And you LOVE your cat Moo." And I started making smoochy noises.

Connor laughed at that. And bought me a pork chop from the vending machine. So everything turned out okay.

I mean, Sam wasn't thrilled with me, I could tell. But he'll bounce back—he always does. And then I'll coach him on how to hang with the creepers.

So now I'm sitting in my room staring at my blank walls, where my posters of Kid Z used to be. I HAD to take them down. I mean, Connor didn't really give me a choice. But if I can't impress him with my serious rap skills, I'm going to have to think of something else.

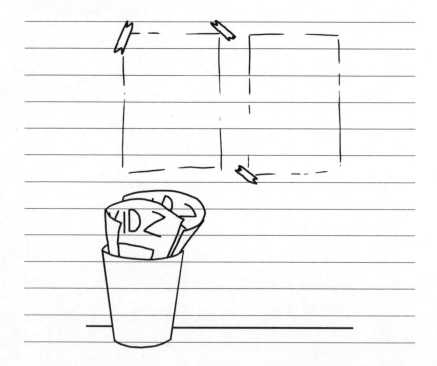

Like . . . DRAWING. My old buddy Cash Creeper
loved to draw as much as I do. If I can whip up some
masterpiece before school tonight, maybe Connor
will be begging for an autographed copy that he can
frame for his own bedroom walls—or at least be a
little impressed.

Yup, that's the ticket. My pencil is itching to draw
already . . .

DAY 3: SATURDAY MORNING

Wow. So that creeper is NOT easily impressed.

I worked all day on a bunch of drawings. I barely got any sleep at all.

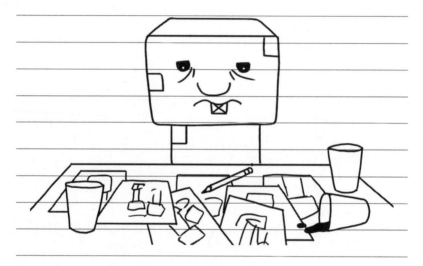

And when I showed up at school last night, I pulled out my journal and pretended like I was finishing up one of the drawings right there in Language Arts—before the bell rang.

Connor came in. And do you know what he said? He said really loud-like, "What's THAT? Your coloring book?"

Chloe snickered from the desk on the other side of him, which I really didn't appreciate. Then she started telling Connor all about Strategic Exploding class, babbling on and on like it was the most interesting thing in the world. And me? I put my journal away before Connor thought I really WAS some little kid who was into coloring.

But I mean, if he wasn't into rap and he wasn't into drawing, what WAS he into? Did we have ANYTHING in common?

It didn't hit me until lunchtime, when Sam started showing me another one of his Cat Cam videos.

I watched it because, you know, I hadn't been all that nice to Sam on Thursday night. And there was

Moo batting at her newest toy, a stuffed creeper hanging off fishing rod. RUDE. Couldn't Sam have gotten her a zombie toy? Or a skeleton toy? Nope. She was chasing a little green creeper, whacking at it like she wanted it for lunch.

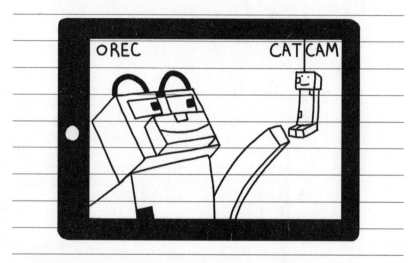

When she finally caught it and dragged it off camera, Ziggy laughed so hard, a chunk of rotten flesh fell out of his mouth. It hit the table in front of me with a SPLAT.

GROSS.

Then Connor sat down and asked us what we were watching. And Sam could hardly wait to show him.

Well Connor took one look at that screen, and he flipped over backward in his chair. Seriously. He landed FLAT on his back. I thought he was going to blow sky high!

See, it turns out that Connor and I DO have something in common. We both hate cats. In fact, he might hate them even more than me. He told Sam to shut that video off and never play it again. EVER.

And even though Sam looked like a squished slime ball, I had to kind of back up Connor on this one. If you're gonna hang out with creepers, you can't be showing cat videos all the time. It's just not cool.

By the time I got home this morning, I was feeling a whole lot better about my 30-Day Plan. Connor wasn't into rap or drawing, but he'd probably be ALL OVER flinging mushrooms at Sir Coughs-a-Lot. It was a start anyway.

When another rap popped into my head, I decided to write it down, even if Connor didn't want to hear it.

Moo, Moo, Moo, Mitty, Moo, Moo, Moo,
Sam likes cats and witches, too.

Shares a kiss and mushroom stew with
Moo, Moo, Moo, Mitty, Moo, Moo, Moo.

DAY 3: SATURDAY NIGHT

Sam invited me to a sleepover tonight, but I had to say no. See, I'm trying to make some progress on my plan. How can I stick close to Connor if I don't know where he lives or what he does on the weekends?

So I invited Sam to the Creeper Café in town instead. I figured it was as good a place as any to run into Connor. Plus, I'm trying to coach Sam in how to play it cool around creepers. At the Creeper Café, he can watch other creepers in action. It's like a big science experiment.

We sat in a booth at the café and tried to keep a low profile. And I ordered us two super-deluxe hot chocolates with whipped cream and sprinkles—my favorite.

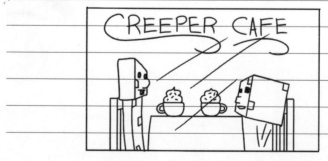

But I forgot two VERY important things:

1. Sam probably shouldn't have caffeine. It gives him the jitters, and a jittery, wiggly slime is a totally out of control slime. I could practically FEEL the booth shaking.

2. Sam is lactose intolerant. I KNOW he shouldn't drink milk. Like EVER. But I forgot whipped cream has milk in it. So . . . well, we had to clear out of there fast.

And just as we were running out the door—Sam all wobbly and hyped up on caffeine—guess who walked in?

Yup. Connor. The first thing he said was, "Hey, Gerald!" He remembered my name, which is a good sign. And he seemed happy to see me.

The next thing he said was, "Holy stink. What's that smell?"

That's when Sam got all wiggly and embarrassed and said, "Yeah, that'd be me. Sorry about that."

He actually ADMITTED that he caused that disgusting smell. Who DOES that? I could think of a gazillion other things to say, like "I think some critter died in the walls" or "Someone probably lit off a firecracker" or "There's a baby zombie in the corner booth who needs a serious diaper change."

But Sam's too honest. And he's not that quick of a thinker, even when he's all caffeined up.

Connor got as far away from us as FAST as he could. Then Sam bounced out the door as if nothing had happened. And I followed him out feeling like something DID die in the walls—my hope for a friendship with Connor.

R.I.P
Creeper
BFFs

I'm trying to help Sam out—I really am. I mean, it'd be great if we could all three be friends.

But that stinky slime is SURE not making it easy for me!

DAY 6: TUESDAY

So I just got home from school, and I'm DYING to talk to Mom. But there's this note on the table that says she's at the knitting store buying more yarn. MORE yarn? How many scarves, hats, socks, sweaters, and ponchos can one creeper mom knit?

Anyway, I've been pacing my bedroom floor waiting for her to get home. See, there was this big announcement at school last night about a field trip. NEXT week. To Mushroom Island.

The island sounds AWESOME. You have to take a boat to get there, and the island is full of these crazy red and white cows. They're called "Mooshrooms" because red mushrooms grow right on their backs! And we're going to learn how to milk them and all kinds of weird stuff.

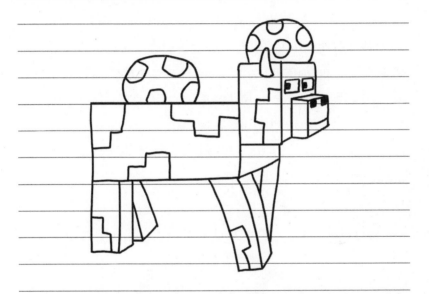

But the best part is that Connor is going. So I HAVE to go too—that's all part of my plan. If I stick with him, he'll get used to having me around. Pretty soon, he'll start thinking of me as his friend—even if he's not into rap and drawing. Even if I have this other friend who is a giant slime, and kind of stinky.

So all I need is Mom's signature on the permission slip, and I'm good to go.

Wait! I hear the front door opening. Be right back . . .

Life is SO unfair.

Do you know what Mom said when I asked her about Mushroom Island? She said that Mooshrooms carry DISEASE. She said that I could get something called "Mad Mooshroom Disease" from those cows. REALLY??? Sometimes I think all that knitting is knotting up Mom's brain, too.

MAD MOOSHROOM DISEASE

I told her that the school wouldn't be taking us to the island if it were even a teensy bit dangerous. But she said that it was a PARENT'S job to keep her creeper kids safe. And that there would be other kids staying back next week too. And that they'd all be impressed by the new sweater I'd be wearing, just as soon as she could unravel the yarn she'd bought.

Well, I paced my room again until Dad got home. I figured HE could talk some sense into Mom. But he didn't! He took one look at the mound of yarn on the kitchen table, and he pretty much ran for the backyard, as if he could outrun the new sweater Mom would be making for HIM.

"Dad," I said. "Wait! Can I go on the field trip to Mushroom Island?"

"Whatever your mother says, Gerald." That was the last thing I heard before the back door slammed shut. End of discussion.

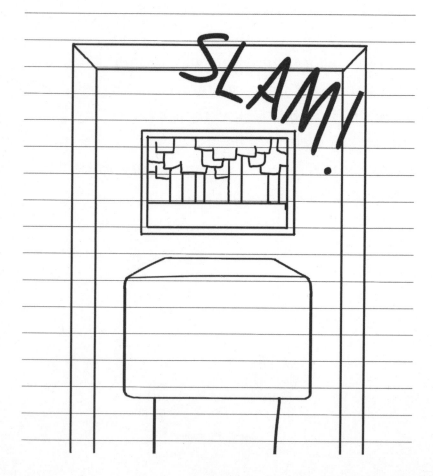

So . . . I guess Connor is going on the field trip without me. He'll probably end up hanging with some of the other older creepers. And he'll have a blast. And forget all about Gerald Creeper Jr.

But, hey. At least I'll get a new sweater out of the deal!

GREAT.

DAY 7: WEDNESDAY

So something really interesting happened last night—WAY more interesting than a new sweater.

Actually, it happened this morning after school. See, I was about to walk home when I saw Connor standing behind the school watching the Spider Riding class. I hoped he wasn't thinking about joining THAT. I mean, it's all jocks in the class—spider jockeys like Bones and his buddies.

In fact, right as I was walking over to say that to Connor, Bones rode by on this big hairy spider. I

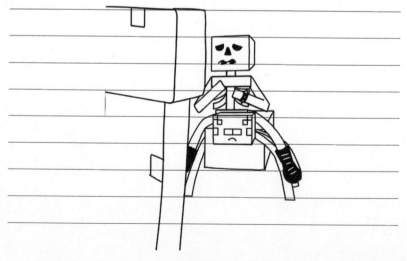

don't even like to look at them, with their red eyes and furry bodies. But Connor stared right at that spider. He even kind of stepped into its path.

I expected Bones to take some kind of crack at Connor, the way he always does with me. But he didn't. He just backed his spider up, as if it were HIS bad that Connor nearly got run over. And he rode the other way.

WEIRD.

I was going to ask Connor about it, but that was right about the time he asked ME something. He asked if I was going on the field trip.

It killed me to tell him no. I mean, he was practically inviting me to go WITH him, and I had to say that Mom was keeping me safe from Mad Mooshroom Disease. Well, I didn't really say that. I mean, I need Connor to think I'm a normal kid from a normal creeper family. In other words, I have to lie.

So I said that I'd forgotten to get my parents'
signature. The permission slips are due tomorrow
(that part's true), and I said my parents were out of
town tonight. Oh, well. Too bad for me.

That's when Connor said he had an idea. He looked
around like he didn't want anyone else to hear it.

But my Evil Twin showed up to wreck the day. She
sprinted toward us from a nearby field and said,
"Hey, Connor. Are you here to join Strategic
Exploding?"

"Nope," he said. "Not a chance." Then he turned
back to me as if she were nothing more than a pesky
silverfish.

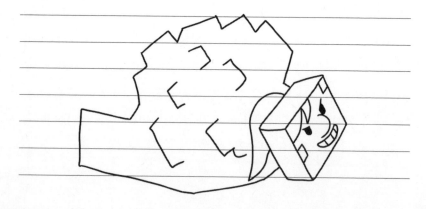

Well, she wasn't happy about that. I saw her face darken, the way it does when she's thinking about exploding. She didn't do it right away. But then Connor turned around and said, "Are you still here? Give us some space, would ya? This is a guy thing."

That did it. There's nothing Chloe hates worse than being left out.

She set her jaw, scrunched her eyes shut, and strategically exploded. And as Connor and I shook the gunpowder off, he rolled his eyes and said, "GIRLS."

"Yeah, I know, right?" I said, hoping he'd get back to sharing his big idea.

And maybe he would have. But Sam bounced over right about then with his girlfriend, Willow. "Hey guys!" he said all perky like. (See, I told you he'd bounce back.) "What are you talking about?"

"Guy stuff," I explained. Even though I had no idea what that meant.

Willow turned her ear toward us, as if she had brewed some Potion of Better Hearing and wanted to hear every word of this Guy Stuff.

But Connor picked right up on that. He pulled Sam in closer. "Can you tell your girlfriend we need a little privacy here?"

"What do you mean?" asked Sam, confused. "It's after school. Willow and I ALWAYS hang out after school."

Connor flashed me a look of disgust. "Dude, grow a backbone," he said to Sam. And he started hissing, which meant I was running out of time to hear his big idea.

"SAM," I whispered. "Tell Willow to go away."

Well that did it. I don't think slimes have a single bone in their bodies, but all of a sudden, he managed to grow one. He stood up tall and walked away. Or bounced away. Next to his girlfriend.

"Okay, so where were we?" asked Connor.

"Guy stuff. Big idea," I reminded him.

"Right." He got that gleam back in his eye and told me that he made a bunch of fireworks to take to Mooshroom Island.

Fireworks? I LOVE fireworks! And if Connor did *too,* that meant we had ANOTHER thing in common.

But then I remembered something. I wasn't going on that field trip!

When I reminded him of that, he got another big idea. "I'll sign your *permission slip,*" he said. "Seeing as how your parents are out of town and all. I have pretty stellar penmanship." He flashed that grin again—the one he gave Mrs. Collins. I think he probably gets away with a lot of stuff because of that "Who me? I'm just an innocent creeper!" smile.

But now I had a decision to make:

- · Have Connor sign the permission slip. Go on the field trip (even though I might make Mom mad—and catch Mad Mooshroom Disease). And set off fireworks with Connor Creeper, my new best friend.

OR

· Stay home from the field trip. Forget the fireworks. And wear an itchy new sweater.

Well, *hmm. That was a toughie.*

So that's how I ended up sitting at *home* this morning with a signed *permission slip.*

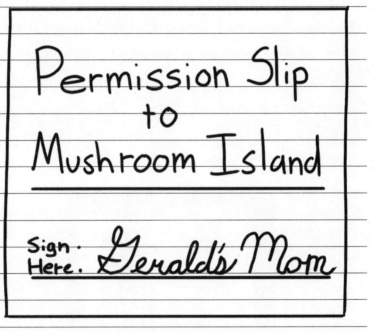

I don't have all the details worked out yet, but I'm getting there. So far, my 30-day plan is shaping right up. Did I mention I'm pretty good at this planning thing?

DAY 9: FRIDAY

Did you know you can use Cat Cams for something GOOD?

While Sam was wasting his precious camera taking videos of Moo batting at water, running into windows, and dressed up in dumb little costumes, Connor was catching way more interesting video. Turns out, he's been using a camera to spy on Bones. Which explains a LOT.

See, after school this morning, I saw Bones steer clear of Connor again. And I finally got up the nerve to ask Connor about it.

"What gives?" I asked. "Bones doesn't like creepers. But he likes you. Or at least he leaves you alone, which is even BETTER than him liking you."

And Connor said that the secret to a good relationship with a skeleton is getting some dirt on him.

He didn't mean like the blocks of dirt you get from the ground. He meant like BLACKMAIL—like what you see in movies.

I guess Bones has been secretly riding the school's spiders over the weekend. Which is REALLY illegal. I mean, if he gets caught, he might get thrown in jail. (Or at least kicked off the Spider Jockey team.)

And somehow, Connor caught it on video last weekend. He was passing by the school and saw it all, and just happened to have his camera with him. And once Bones found out Connor had "dirt" on him, he started treating him really well.

So just when I thought Connor couldn't get any cooler, he went and did.

COOL LEVELS

I'm wishing I had some dirt on Bones too. But maybe if I stick close to Connor, Bones will leave me alone. So far, so good, right?

DAY 11: SUNDAY

The field trip is TOMORROW NIGHT. If I were
anything like my Evil Twin or Cammy the Exploding
Baby, I'd blow up with excitement. But I'm also
really nervous—like itchy-skin nervous. See, when
I'm even the SLIGHTEST bit nervous, I sweat. And
sweating makes my skin itch.

So do ugly wool sweaters. But lucky me! Mom just
finished a new one for me tonight. "You can wear

it to school tomorrow," she said. "It'll be just like you're on that field trip!"

I didn't know what she meant until I studied the sweater. It was green and had these red and white things on it. Was it a Christmas sweater? Nope. It was a MUSHROOM sweater.

Those red and white things were mushrooms. SERIOUSLY? If I ever wore that thing, I'd look like I'd caught Mad Mooshroom Disease for sure.

I wanted to run for the hills—or at least the backyard, like Dad does. But Mom looked SO proud. So I put it on so Mom could take a picture to send to Aunt Constance. I sort of think they have a competition going to see who can knit the ugliest things. Mom's GOT to be winning this one.

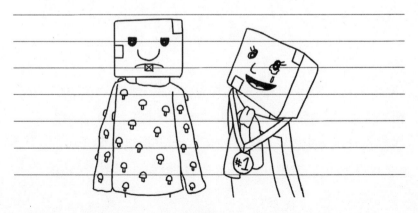

That's when my older sister, Cate, walked into the room. She's kind of moody and doesn't smile very often. I think it's because Dad made her break up with a miner named Steve, and she hasn't been right ever since. But when she saw me in the sweater with mushrooms on it, she just about flipped her wig laughing.

See, I call my sister the Fashion Queen because she wears all these weird wigs and dresses up in crazy costumes. I don't think she's really one to judge my mushroom sweater. I mean, like tonight—she was wearing *this* purple villager robe, like she was a priest or something. Where does she GET this stuff? Her closet is stuffed full of it.

Mom took Cate's laughter as a sign that she LIKED the sweater. And Mom said she'd knit Cate one, too. Well that shut my sister right up.

When she protested, I took the opportunity to escape to my room and bury the sweater under my bed.

And tomorrow? I'll have to hide that sweater as soon as i'm out the front door.

But I have more important things to think about right now. Like how I'm going to score a seat next to Connor on the boat ride to Mushroom Island. And whether I should pack a few fireworks of my own.

We have a whole barrel of gunpowder in the garage—mostly from Cammy's explosions. And if

I start now, I can make a few fireworks before morning. THAT would impress Connor for sure, right?

I'd better get started!

DAY 13: TUESDAY

Dad says the number 13 is unlucky. I think he might be right. Because on Day 13 of my 30-Day Plan, things started to fall apart—or should I say started to BLOW apart.

But let me start at the beginning.

As soon as Chloe and I got to school last night, she headed toward the gym. See, the kids who weren't going on the field trip got to spend the morning

either in the gym OR in the art room. PERFECT! My
Evil Twin would think I was off creating art—not
riding a boat to Mushroom Island. I made a point of
telling Chloe where I was going, which I never do.
"I'm heading off to art now!" I hollered after her
down the hall.

"Good for you," Chloe said. "See you later."

Okay. Done. THAT was the easy part of the day.

The boat ride to Mushroom Island went alright too.

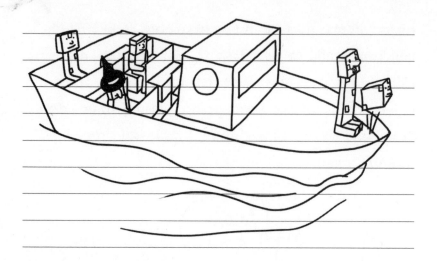

I mean, I kind of had to bounce Sam out of the
seat next to me. I told him it really wasn't big
enough for a slime like him—that he should find a
seat with more elbow room. He doesn't actually
HAVE elbows. But the thing about Sam is, he
doesn't think about things like that. He just said
"Thanks, Gerald" and bounced off happily to sit
somewhere else.

Then I invited Connor to sit by me. He was on his
way over when the eighth-grade boat went by and
Eddy Enderman looked at us. I was kind of surprised
to see him on the boat, because Eddy HATES water.

I tried not to look at his purple eyes. I mean, an Enderman that hates water shouldn't be teleporting around in the middle of it, right?

But Connor didn't know all that. He stared right at Eddy, like he was challenging him. I saw Eddy's eyes narrow with anger. But he didn't teleport and do any damage to Connor—no, Eddy knows how to play it cool. He just looked away first. And Connor gave me this smug smile, as if he'd won some sort of battle.

Some day, I'm going to have to tell him about Eddy.
But for today, I was just happy to be sitting by him.
See, I had something to show him.

I slid my backpack over and whispered, "Take a
look."

He opened up the zipper and peered inside.
"Is that a sweater?" he said. "Wait, are those
MUSHROOMS on your sweater?"

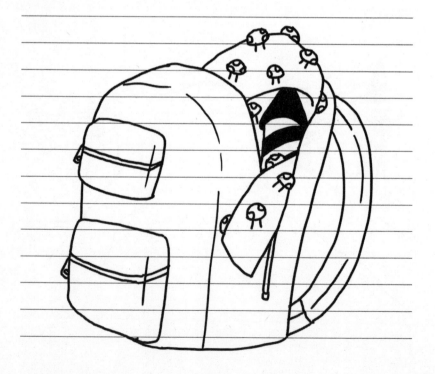

"No!" I said, yanking back my bag. "I mean, look at what's underneath." I pushed the sweater aside, wishing I could toss it overboard. And then I showed Connor the red-and-white-striped rockets I'd made out of paper and gunpowder.

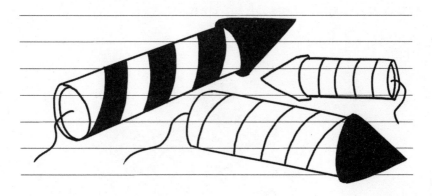

They were decent fireworks, considering I hadn't made any in a while. And I was pretty proud of them—just like Mom was of her mushroom sweater. But Ziggy happened to be staggering by right at that moment, and HE saw the rockets too.

"Whoa," he moaned. "I wish I had fireworks like that." He wiped the drool off his chin.

But Connor just kind of shrugged.

"Cool," he said. "We can add *them to mine.*"

When I looked in HIS backpack, I sucked in my breath. I mean, his rockets were BULGING with gunpowder. Turns out, that creeper has some rocket-making skills of his own.

I could hardly wait to get to the island so we could set them off over the water. How far would they go? Would they make it back to shore?

I wasn't totally sure how we were going to sneak the rockets past Mr. Zane, our sixth-grade chaperone. But Connor is pretty clever—and zombies like Mr. Zane are pretty slow. So, we'd find a way.

As soon as we landed on Mushroom Island, we could hear the Mooshrooms mooing. Then, in the moonlight, we saw their red heads popping up over a hill. They were staring at us, like we were mobs from a faraway land. I guess we kind of were.

Mushroom Island is really hilly, and it's covered in red mushrooms—big ones, little ones, and medium-sized ones. I saw a Mooshroom grazing on a mushroom, and I suddenly heard Mom's voice in my head. "You are what you eat." Here on Mushroom Island, it's really true.

Mr. Zane told us to follow him uphill so he could teach us how to milk a Mooshroom. GROSS. I wasn't having any part of that—until he said that when you milk a Mooshroom with a bowl, you actually get mushroom stew. My stomach kind of growled then. Did I mention I could barely eat dinner last night because I was so nervous? And that I'm a big fan of mushroom stew?

It took a while for Mr. Zane to "catch" a Mooshroom. (Mooshrooms are slow, but zombies are even slower.)

But he finally got that bowl under the Mooshroom and started milking. I could smell the mushroom stew from where I was standing a few feet away, and my mouth started to water.

While he filled that bowl, Mr. Zane told us that you can actually shear the mushrooms off a Mooshroom. "But you don't want to," he said. "Because they don't grow back. And then baby Mooshrooms don't recognize their mothers."

Baby Mooshrooms? Sure enough, one popped out of the herd of Mooshrooms that was grazing beside us on the hilltop. It wandered over on wobbly legs to get a drink from its mother. Now, I'm not big on baby ocelots or baby wolves like some mobs are. But that baby Mooshroom was REALLY cute. Like Cat Cam cute.

Sam was oohing and ahing over that thing as if it were Moo herself. That's when Mr. Zane pulled some wheat out of his pocket and handed it to Sam. He said that if Sam held out the wheat, the baby Mooshroom would follow him. And sure enough, it did!

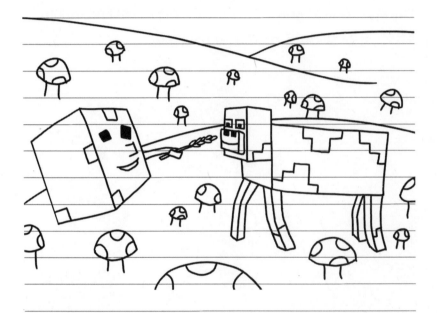

I kind of lost track of Connor for a minute, because I was so into that baby Mooshroom. Sam and I led it down the hill and back up again.

But as we were walking back toward the herd of Mooshrooms, something EXPLODED. At first, I

thought it was Chloe. But then I remembered my
Evil Twin was back at Mob Middle School.

When a rocket lit up the night sky, I knew exactly
what had happened. But why didn't Connor wait
for me? And why would you set off a rocket in the
MIDDLE of a herd of Mooshrooms?

Well they mooed like the Overworld was ending.
And they scattered off that hilltop faster than an
Enderman can teleport.

By the time Sam and I got to Mr. Zane, there wasn't a Mooshroom left in sight—and he had a bowl of mushroom stew dripping off his face. UH-OH. He was one mad zombie.

I looked around for Connor, but he was long gone. Apparently he's good at sneaking away, just like my dad. That's one skill I REALLY have to learn.

Well Mr. Zane made us all march right back to the boat. Then he asked which one of us brought fireworks.

Yup, you know where this is going.

I stayed quiet, but Ziggy Zombie opened his mouth. (I mean, his mouth is pretty much ALWAYS hanging open, right?) He said that Mr. Zane should see the fireworks in MY backpack. I think he was trying to pay me a compliment—not get me in trouble. But that's proof that the zombies should pretty much leave the thinking to us creepers.

So Mr. Zane busted ME for having fireworks, even though I hadn't set a SINGLE ONE of them off.

Not fair! And where was Connor during all this? I don't know. He finally showed up walking along the shoreline, whistling—with NO backpack. I guess he had destroyed the evidence somewhere.

After Mr. Zane lectured me on having respect for critters, Connor crept over and told me not to worry about it. "That was FUN," he said. "Did you see those Mooshrooms run for the hills?"

I didn't really say much, but when I looked up, Eddy Enderman was standing right in front of us. He totally ignored Connor, but he stared right at me.

Be your own Creeper, man. Stay cool.

And then he was gone.

What did he mean by that? I didn't know. But Connor was suddenly looking at me the way I'd been looking at him for the last two weeks. With RESPECT.

"So you know Eddy?" he said.

"Sure," I said. "I mean, his real name is Louis. But that's kind of a secret he shared with me." I don't know why I threw that last part in there. Probably just to prove to Connor that Eddy and I were friends—at least SORT of friends. And I scored some big points with Connor, I could tell.

That should have felt great. I had finally shown Connor how awesome I was (thanks to Eddy Enderman)!

But I didn't really feel like being around him right now. In fact, I didn't even care if he sat by me on the boat ride home. Because all I could think about was the TROUBLE I was going to be in.

Mr. Zane was the least of my worries. It was MOM that a creeper really had to worry about. Good thing I hadn't thrown that mushroom sweater overboard. I was going to have to wear it every day, just to try to get back on Mom's good side.

When we got back to shore this morning, Mr. Zane told me he'd be having a talk with my parents. "I'll be calling them," he promised.

GREAT.

That means I won't get a wink of sleep today. Or if I do, I'll be having daymares about angry Mooshrooms and itchy sweaters.

So, yeah. Day 13 was not a good one in my overall plan. But as Mom always says, the sun will go down again tomorrow. So, I've just gotta cross my feet and hope that I won't be grounded for the rest of my life.

Am I still grounded?

For the rest of your life, Gerald J. Creeper!

DAY 14: WEDNESDAY

YIKES.

Never make your mom mad when she's holding a pair of knitting needles.

I thought she was going to knit a giant spider web and wrap me up in it so that I'd never, ever be able to leave the house again.

She probably would have, except she ran out of yarn—AGAIN.

So instead, she made me hand over my fireworks. And she said I had to write an apology letter to Mr. Zane and the whole sixth grade class.

I thought about Connor Creeper and that smile he uses to charm teachers and get out of trouble. I tried that smile tonight.

And I decided to share a couple of interesting facts about Mooshrooms with Mom, too—just to prove that the field trip hadn't been a total waste of time.

"Mom, did you know that you can shear the mushrooms right off a Mooshroom?"

"Don't interrupt me when I'm punishing you, Gerald," she said.

I looked to Dad for help, but he was wearing this turtleneck that Mom had knit. And the neck was so

high, it pretty much covered his mouth. I don't think
he could have said anything even if he'd wanted to.

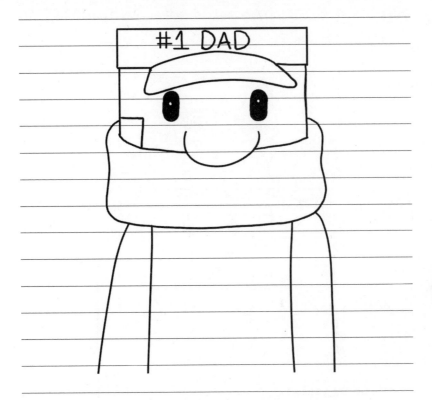

So I just kept talking. "I was thinking, Mom, that
maybe you should get a sheep. And you could shear
the sheep for wool. And never run out of yarn again!"

Dad's eyes got really big when I said that. But Mom
actually stopped to think about it. Genius, right?

Then she caught on to what I was doing and marched me off to my room without dinner. I could smell the burnt pork chops and roasted potatoes from my room, which was REALLY unfair.

The more my stomach growled, the more mad I got at Ziggy Zombie for ratting me out to Mr. Zane. So when I sat down to write that apology letter, I came up with something else instead.

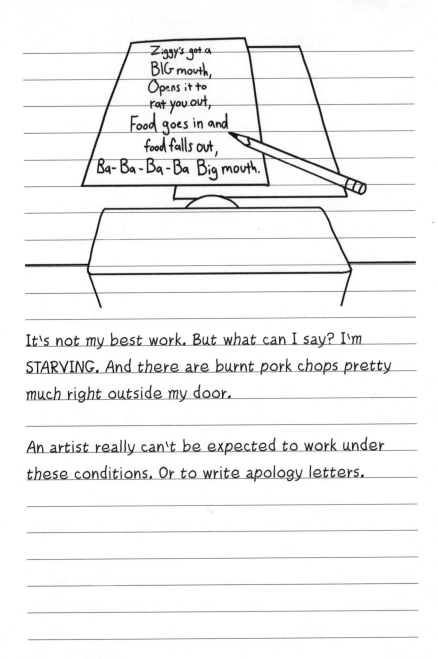

It's not my best work. But what can I say? I'm STARVING. And there are burnt pork chops pretty much right outside my door.

An artist really can't be expected to work under these conditions. Or to write apology letters.

DAY 15: THURSDAY

I'm supposed to go straight TO school and straight HOME from school. Those are Mom's rules.

So when Connor asked me to hang out after school this morning, I said no. It wasn't easy. I mean, I've been wanting to be friends with this guy for two straight weeks now.

But I'm still kind of peeved that he let me take the fall for his fireworks show on Mushroom Island. PLUS I'm grounded. So I told him maybe another time.

"That's too bad," he said. "I'm planning a big adventure tomorrow after school. I thought you'd be just the guy to go with me."

Huh? What am I supposed to do with THAT information?

When I didn't say anything, he said, "It'll take like half an hour. No big deal. Just think about it. Talk to you tomorrow."

Then he crept off, as if HE were the one who had someplace to be.

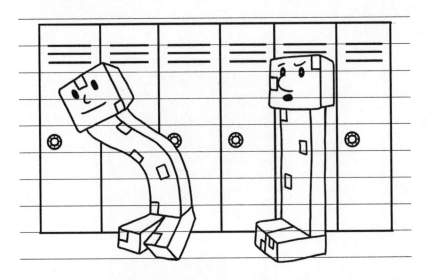

I thought about it on my walk home. An adventure? With Connor? I wondered if it would be like the adventures Cash and I used to take to the swamp. Or to a village nearby, where we'd spy on villager kids.

But Connor's adventure was only going to take half an hour. So . . . I figured I could probably squeeze that in. Even while I'm grounded. I mean, how could I say no?

By the time I got home, I'd made up my mind.
That was when I heard the sheep bleat from the
backyard.

That's right. A SHEEP. In the backyard. Mom was out
there trying to shear it, but it looked like Dad was
taking the brunt of it all. I'm pretty sure he got a
good kick in the kneecaps.

"That's no sheep," he grumbled as he pushed
past me into the house. "That's a wolf in sheep's
clothing."

I don't know what he meant by that. But the sheep
DID look pretty grumpy.

And by the time Mom came in with a bucket full of white wool, she did, too. "That sheep was YOUR idea, mister," she said. "So you're going to help me take care of it."

I decided that the first order of business would be to come up with a name for IT. So I went out to meet the sheep and get a better sense of its personality. I did pretty well with my pet squid. I named him "Sticky," and he's definitely a squid that likes to stick around, staring at me from behind the glass.

"Take Cammy with you," said Mom as I headed outside. "But don't let her near the sheep."

REALLY?

Everyone knows that Cammy's going to want to be near the sheep. And Cammy ALWAYS gets what she wants—or she blows sky high.

Maybe Mom was still punishing me for the Mushroom Island thing. But, whatever. I led my baby sister out into the grass and hoped for the best.

That poor sheep looked so NAKED! He had this white woolly head, but his body was tan where Mom had shaved all his wool off. "You know what you need, buddy?" I asked. "You need a PONCHO. It would cover all your bare parts, and you could stick your head through the hole in the middle."

He bleated. I guess he agreed with me.

Then an idea struck—PONCHO would be the perfect name! I said so out loud. But Cammy shook her head.

"Sock," she said pointing toward one of the sheep's legs.

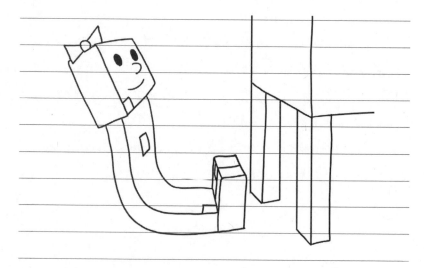

"You want to name the sheep SOCK?" I asked.

She nodded. So that's how the naked sheep in our backyard got its name. But I wasn't about to try to put socks on it. I was going to learn from Dad's mistake and keep my distance.

Sock kept trying to jump the fence between our yard and the neighbor's. But he couldn't get high enough.

And then Sir Coughs-a-Lot started strutting across the neighbor's yard, TEASING Sock about the fact that he couldn't get into that yard.

See? That's why I don't like cats. They give off WAY too much attitude. Where's a mushroom to fling when you need one?

Anyway, it's time for bed, and I'm not tired. So I'm TRYING to count sheep. I've heard that helps. You're supposed to like imagine them jumping over fences in your mind, and count each one as it jumps. But MY sheep can't make it over the fence. So counting Sock isn't going to get me anywhere.

1 Sheep...

Instead, I'm going to imagine Connor's "big adventure" tomorrow. Maybe it'll be something good—something SO fun I'll forget all about Mushroom Island. And Connor and I will come out of it buddies. This could be our big breakthrough!

I can see it now: Connor and me skydiving high above the Overworld. Or sledding down hills in the Taiga. Or battling the Ender Dragon side by side. I mean, none of that is probably going to happen in half an hour. But what can I say?

A creeper's gotta have dreams.

DAY 16: FRIDAY

So THAT'S IT. I'm going to jail.

Any minute now, the creeper cops are going to come pick me up and throw me behind bars. Slam the door shut and throw away the key.

I mean, I should have KNOWN it would come to this! Dad told me a few months ago that I come from a long line of convicts. At least one anyway: a great uncle on Dad's side who blew up a village well. I saw his mug shot myself, clipped out of the Creeper Chronicle.

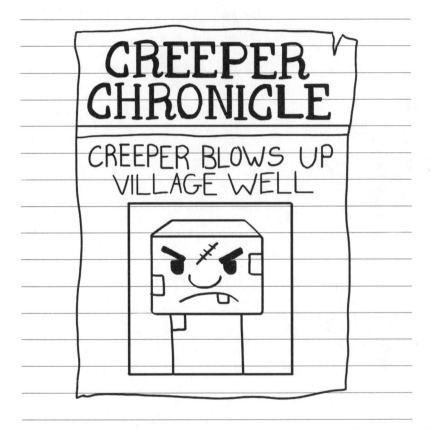

The minute I saw the photo of my Convict Creeper Uncle, I should have turned my life around. I should have thrown on a purple robe like Cate's and joined the priesthood in the nearest village.

But I didn't. Instead, I tried to buddy up to some creep named Connor. And now my life is over. O. V. E. R.

I might as well practice my confession now.

You see, officers, I stole a few emeralds. Yup, right out of the school vending machine. I didn't MEAN to. I guess I was more like the lookout guy. But I didn't know what was happening!

It all went down like this: Connor met me after school, and he said I was in for a real treat. We tiptoed back into the school after everyone left, and Connor made me stand in the hall watching for the janitor.

But the janitor is this half-asleep zombie, so I wasn't even worried. Until I heard the PLINK, PLINK, PLINK of emeralds dropping out of the vending machine behind me.

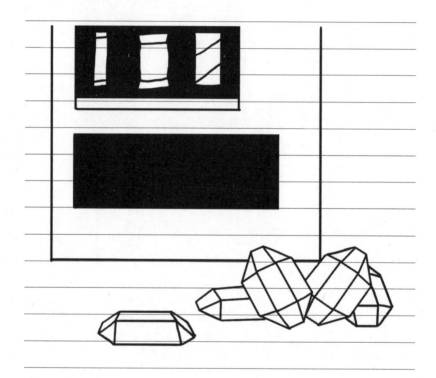

I guess that old janitor is SO slow, Connor stole the key to the vending machine from him! And he didn't even know.

So THAT's where Connor has been getting all his emeralds for the vending machine. He's been getting them FROM the vending machine!

As soon as he'd filled up his sack, we made a run for it. And let me tell you, I've never run so fast in all my life—not even when I took Sprinting as an extracurricular. We parted ways when we got outside. We didn't even talk about it. I just wanted to get as far away from that creep as I could.

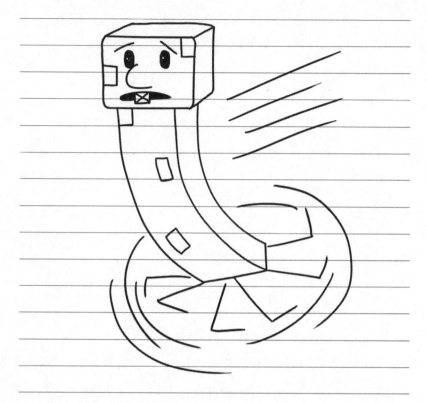

Now I think I know what Dad meant when he said
Sock was a "wolf in sheep's clothing." Connor may
LOOK like a creeper, just like me and my old buddy
Cash. But the dude is a total poser. It's like he's
just wearing a creeper skin—like villager kids do on
Halloween. Because inside? He's more like Bones
and his skeleton buddies. He's a liar and a robber,
and he's NO friend of mine.

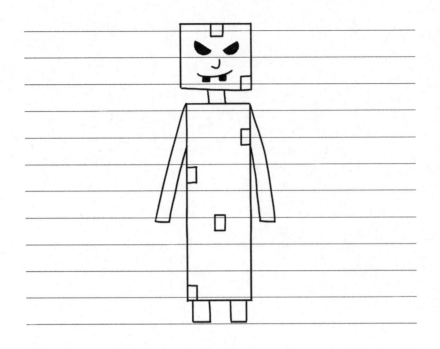

Except that's not going to really hold up down
at the police station. "Not your friend?" the
creeper cops are going to ask me. "That's not what
everyone at Mob Middle School says. That's not
what your JOURNAL says." Yup, they'll have it in my
very own handwriting. I should probably just burn my
journal now.

So I'm sitting here in my bedroom sweating. And
ITCHING. And panicking. I really don't want my mug

shot posted in the Creeper Chronicle. I REALLY don't want to go to jail.

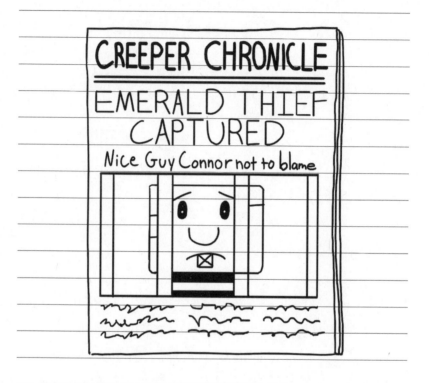

But the law's the law. The most I can hope for is visiting hours at the prison so Mom can bring me a roasted pork chop now and then . . .

DAY 17: SATURDAY

Mom made me go to school last night. I told her that since I was still grounded, I really didn't DESERVE to go to school. I said I should probably just stay locked in my room all night until I learned my lesson. (Or until I got used to living in a four by four foot room, because that's pretty much how I'm going to spend the rest of my life as a Convict Creeper.)

But Mom wasn't having it. So SOMEHOW, I crept my way back into that school—to the scene of the crime. But I had to walk around that place like I had eyes in the back of my head. Like EVERYONE was watching me. Like I might get apprehended by the school security cop at any moment.

When Connor showed up, I couldn't even look at him. And when he offered to buy me something from the vending machine, I was like, "SERIOUSLY?" The dude has no shame.

In fact, *he asked me if I wanted to go on ANOTHER adventure*—something about planting fireworks in the Strategic Exploding field outside. I didn't even hear him out. I just said "No." Actually, I said "NO way. No how. Not happening. Leave me alone. I'm outta here."

But he FOLLOWED me. All the way to Language Arts class. I mean, he was going there anyway, but I could feel him creeping on my heels. Breathing down my neck. I started to sweat again.

Eddy Enderman passed us in the hall, and I saw him glance my way. I almost shot him a plea for help with my eyeballs, but then I reached Mrs. Collins's classroom and ducked inside there instead.

"Dude, what is your problem?" Connor hissed.

"YOU," I said—too loud. "You're my problem."

Well Mrs. Collins caught wind of that and took us both out into the hall. But when she asked what was going on, Connor plastered on his "I'm all innocent" look. And do you know what he said? He said that he'd been TRYING to make friends with me for the last two weeks, because you know—I'm the only other boy creeper in sixth grade. But he said that I don't want to be friends with him. That I've been treating him like a silverfish stuck to the bottom of my shoe.

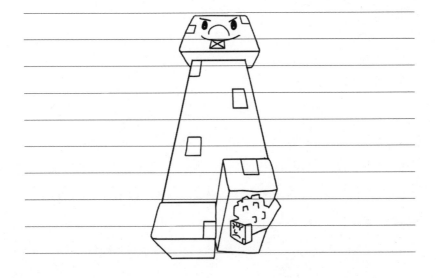

WHAT? I couldn't believe what I was hearing.

But Mrs. Collins believed it—every last word. "Gerald Creeper," she said in THAT tone. You know the one. "I'm really disappointed in you. It's hard to be the new creep at school. So I want to see you making more of an effort to be a friend to Connor, do you understand? Starting with class today. You two will be partners during our creative writing lesson. Got it?"

What I "got" was a sudden stomachache—as if Mad Mooshroom Disease was coming on all quick-like. I told Mrs. Collins that I should probably go to the nurse's office. But she said I was faking it and that I could just sit right down next to my partner.

REALLY? So she knows that I'M faking it, but she can't see that Connor is a total poser? I think Mrs. Collins ought to get her glasses checked.

As I shuffled back into the classroom, I caught Eddy Enderman's eye again. He'd been watching the whole scene from his locker down the hall. And by the look on his face, I could tell that HE believed me. Sometimes I think Eddy Enderman is the only one at school who really knows what's going on. I just wish he could DO something about it! Oh, well. Maybe he can bust me out of jail someday—teleport me right out of there, and I can live out the rest of my life hiding in the Nether.

So now I'm supposed to be working with Connor on creative writing. But I'm writing in my journal instead. And he's copying Chloe's poem. And she's LETTING him!

Whatever. NOT my problem. I'm done with Connor Creeper.

DAY 20: TUESDAY MORNING

I may be done with Connor Creeper. But he's not done with me. NOT AT ALL.

Do you know what happened right after Language Arts class? I discovered that my journal was MISSING. I thought I had put it in my backpack. In fact, I'm sure I did. But when I checked again in second period, it was gone—like it had sprouted legs and just walked away.

Or . . . someone TOOK it. Like my "partner," Connor Creeper.

My journal was gone all weekend. It was so WEIRD not to have it. I felt like Sock the Sheep without his wool—which is growing back, by the way, in weird little patches.

And you know what? My journal came back too. Mysteriously. Last night. It just showed up on my desk in Language Arts.

I was relieved to see it, let me tell you. But I also had this sick feeling in the pit of my creeper stomach, like I'd eaten a spider eye or something. Because I knew that Connor had read my journal. Cover to cover. Every. Single. Word.

That means he knows exactly how I feel about him right now. And how I feel about every other mob at Mob Middle School. Which is NOT good.

See, Connor and I just went from being almost friends to DEFINITE enemies. And I've seen the kind of pranks that guy can pull on his enemies. I did NOT want to be one of them.

Then I realized on the way to second period that it was already too late. There was this big crowd gathered around Ziggy's locker, which is unusual because it kind of stinks. And at the front of the crowd, Ziggy was reading something out loud that was stuck to his locker.

It was the rap I wrote about him! He read the WHOLE thing, and I swear when he got to the part about food falling out of his mouth, a chunk of something DID hit the hallway floor. But the mobs around him were falling all over themselves laughing.

"Heeeeyyyyyy . . ." said Ziggy, finally realizing that someone was making fun of him. That zombie's not too quick on the uptake. "Who wrote that?"

"It says right here," said some seventh grade witch, pointing at the paper stuck to Ziggy's locker. "Gerald Creeper Jr."

"What?" I faked surprise. "No way. That's not even my handwriting." That part was true—Connor must have copied the rap onto a new sheet of paper in his OWN handwriting.

"Oh yeah?" said the witch. "Then whose handwriting is it?"

I should have said Connor Creeper. But then I caught him staring at me, and he kind of narrowed his eyes. I can't read minds, but if I could, I'm pretty sure he'd be telling me not to say a word. OR ELSE.

See, now that we've held up a vending machine together, he has some dirt on me—even dirtier than the dirt he has on Bones. And did I mention that I REALLY don't want to go to jail? So instead of saying that Connor Creeper wrote the rap, I said the OTHER name that came to mind.

"Sam," I said quickly. "That's Sam's handwriting. In fact, I think I see a slime smudge on the edge of the page."

Well Sam was right beside me. Of course he was—he usually is, which is why he's the first one I throw under the bus whenever I start to panic.

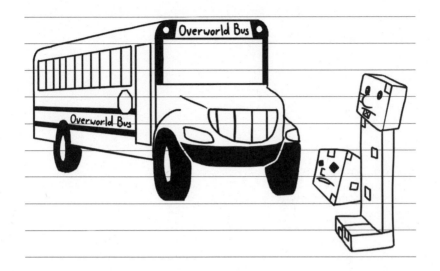

Sam's jolly eyes got wide, and he said, "Really? Let me see that." He pushed his way to the front of the crowd and looked at the paper. "That's not my writing," he said. "See? I don't make my B's like that."

Now I didn't think anyone would believe that Sam actually wrote that rap. He's a TERRIBLE rapper. But as we walked farther down the hall, we ran into another crowd gathered around another locker. And judging by all the skeletons in that crowd, I wasn't surprised to hear Bones's voice rattle out.

"Listen up, Bones,
Sitting on your throne,
You're going down
With a grunt and groan.

"Listen up, yo,
Watch your bony back,
You're going down—whatcha
think about that?"

Bones's voice was pretty much a growl by the time he got done reading. He started cracking his bony knuckles. Then he read the very last line:

GREAT. Just great. Connor had copied every rap out of my journal and was TAKING ME DOWN with my own words.

But then someone said, "Gerald didn't write that. It's SAM'S handwriting!"

"Yeah!" I heard the word come out of my own mouth. And then Sam whirled around and looked at me.

"What? No it's not!" But it was too late.

Bones and his gang surrounded Sam and started throwing him around like a bouncy green ball.

"Hey!" BOUNCE. "Wait!" BOUNCE. "Stop!" BOUNCE.

Sam could barely eek out a few words in between bounces. Luckily, one of the skeletons had bad aim and sent Sam flying sideways down the hall.

He rolled into a tight little ball and kept on rolling, right down the stairs to the first floor of Mob Middle School.

He rolled into a tight little ball and kept on rolling, right down the stairs to the first floor.

But he wasn't speaking to me. AT ALL. Until he found a sheet of paper on HIS locker, too.

He read it out loud:

It was one of my nicer raps, I have to say. I mean, Sam DOES like cats and witches. And he DOES kiss his cat right on the lips. And he shares his mushroom stew with her ALL THE TIME. So on a normal day, Sam would have probably LOVED my rap.

But today wasn't a normal day. Because Sam had just been rolled down the hallway like a bowling ball by Bones and his buddies.

So today, he tore that rap off his locker and said to me, "Are you gonna tell everyone I wrote THAT rap, too?"

It was about as mad as I've ever seen Sam get— except for one time when I said something not so nice about his girlfriend.

And that was the last I saw of him all night. He didn't sit with me at lunch. Ziggy didn't either. Maybe he decided to sit by someone who would actually appreciate all the junk falling out of his mouth.

So I sat by myself at the lunch table for pretty much the first time in my whole Mob Middle School career. And I kept getting nasty looks from other kids. Because there were a LOT of rap songs in my journal. And most of them showed up taped to lockers today.

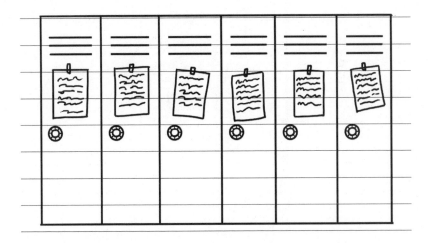

Plus, by lunchtime, the mobs had pretty much figured out that Sam hadn't written a word of those raps. Nope. They were all written by yours truly.

So after lunch, I did something I've never done in my whole life. I skipped out of school. I pretended like I was going to Art class, but I snuck out the door instead. I figure it's only a matter of time before I get busted for the vending machine thing. So I might as well start getting used to a life of crime.

I crept home and slipped through the back door, hoping Sock the Sheep wouldn't bleat out a really loud hello.

And I snuck *past the living room,* where Mom sat on the couch knitting the longest scarf I'd ever seen in my life. It rolled right off the couch and down the hall. I *practically tripped* over it on the way to my room.

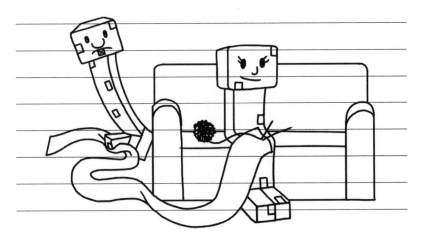

You know, Mom knits ALL the time. But I don't see her getting any happier, so I'm starting to wonder if that book she read was all a scam—if Aunt Constance had sent her down the wrong path, like Connor tried to do with me.

Then again, my life isn't exactly coming up roses, so who am I to judge?

Anyway, I made it to my room without being seen. And now I'm buried under the covers. But I'm keeping one eye out. Because Sticky the Squid is staring at me, and right now, he's probably the only friend I've got.

DAY 21: WEDNESDAY MORNING

"Mom, I have to switch schools."

I said it the moment Chloe walked in the door after Strategic Explosions class. I knew if I didn't, she'd bust me for skipping school. The trick with Chloe is to beat her to the punch.

Mom was standing at the stove burning bacon to a crisp, just the way I like it. And there was syrup or something bubbling on another burner. So maybe she was going to make us a REAL breakfast, which we really haven't had since she started this whole knitting thing.

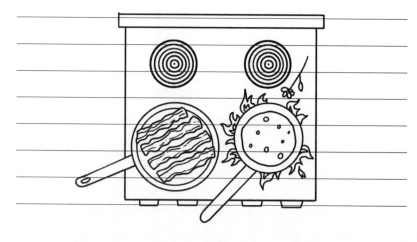

When Mom looked my way, I could tell she was only half listening. She was probably thinking about her next knitting project. PERFECT. Some of my best conversations with her happen when she's not really listening, like when she's cleaning or folding laundry.

"I need to switch schools, Mom. Seriously. Because someone got a hold of my journal—my PRIVATE journal—and spread it all over school. And now all my friends hate me."

"Well don't even THINK about blaming me," said Chloe, snitching a piece of bacon off the plate. I guess she gets in trouble so often, she figures I'm going to try to pin this one on her.

I just ignored her. "I have it all worked out, Mom. There's that private Creeper Academy on the edge of town. I can start on Monday—after a couple of days off to clear my head."

"Okay, dear."

OKAY??? I couldn't believe it. I shot Chloe a look of victory.

Then Mom turned around and added, "But you'll have to find a job to pay for it—that academy is really expensive. Oh, and you'll have to wear a uniform. You know that, right?"

Well, CRUD. I hadn't thought that one totally through. For just a second, I pictured myself hitting up that vending machine ONE LAST TIME to get enough emeralds to pay for Creeper Academy. But it was already a miracle I hadn't been busted after my first robbery. Another one would put me behind bars, for sure.

Plus, there was just no getting around those uniforms at Creeper Academy. I'd seen them before—Cate went to the academy for like a month when she was having trouble at her public school. And I think it was those disgusting uniforms that sent her into her weird Fashion Queen phase.

See, the uniforms are the color of silverfish. And they're really stiff. They actually kind of squeak when you walk in _them_. Personally, I think I'd rather wear prison stripes.

Anyway, after Mom harshed my mellow about Creeper Academy, I decided to put my Life Planning on hold and focus on breakfast. But that "syrup" on the stove turned out to be dye for turning sheep's wool different colors. Mom made it with dandelions. Which means my next sweater is going to be dandelion yellow.

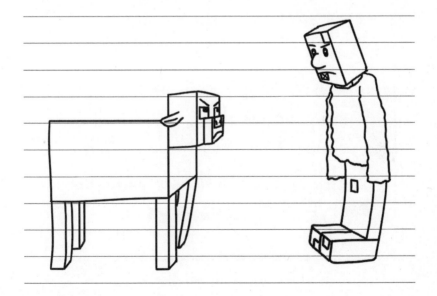

Yup, I really have to come up with a new plan.

PLAN

- Join the priesthood! (It's not too late, right?)

- Embrace a life of crime with Connor. (Yeah, maybe not...)

- Go work on a sheep farm. (Could Sock get me an interview?)

- Make MOM get a job and babysit Cammy for her. (Now you're thinking, Creeper!)

- Build a portal to Nether and never, ever, EVER come back.

Hmm . . . I gotta say, apart from that last one, I'm not really loving my options.

Which is how I ended up agreeing to go back to Mob Middle School tonight.

Wish me luck. This creeper needs all the help he can get.

HELP
WANTED

DAY 22: THURSDAY MORNING

I'm starting to know what it must feel like to be an Enderman. I walked through the halls of Mob Middle School last night and NO ONE looked me in the eye. Not a single mob.

I actually started thinking that maybe I was invisible—like Willow Witch had thrown a splash potion of invisibility over me when I wasn't looking, and mobs really couldn't see me.

By lunchtime, I was ready to ASK her for a potion like that. Because it would feel a lot less lonely if I actually WERE invisible.

But Sam still isn't speaking to me. Which means Willow Witch probably won't speak to me either. I'll bet that if I went over to Sam's house in the swamp, Moo wouldn't even MEOW at me.

I sure tease Sam a lot about all that love stuff,
but he's got two mobs in his corner. How many do I
have?

Zero. Zippo. Nada.

I didn't even see Eddy Enderman last night, and
he's the one mob I was pretty sure would at least
acknowledge me. But then, it was raining out,
which means he probably took a sick night at home.
Endermen really don't like rain.

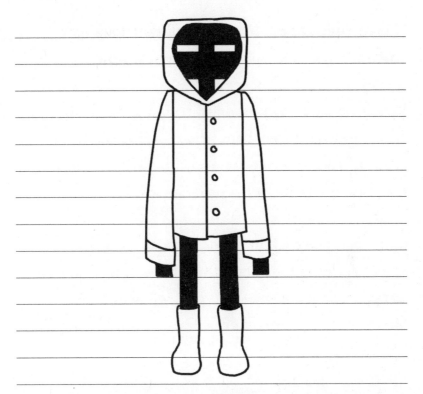

But thinking about Eddy made me remember the last time he spoke to me. It was on Mushroom Island, and he said something like "Be your own creeper, man."

I don't really have a choice now. I'm on my own here at Mob Middle School. But I think Eddy might have meant something different—like maybe I shouldn't let Connor tell me what kind of creeper to be.

Maybe Eddy knew Connor was going to lead me toward a life of crime. He's smart that way.

I really should have listened to Eddy, but I didn't. Sheesh. When I look back at the happy-go-lucky creeper I was two weeks ago, I barely recognize the guy. Boy, did he have things wrong.

So I came home after school this morning, and I saw the strangest thing in the backyard. A YELLOW sheep. A dandelion-yellow-colored sheep. When he bleated at me, I realized it was Sock. But what had Mom DONE to him?

I asked her, and she said she'd dyed his wool. And I was like, "Mom, I think you're supposed to dye the wool AFTER you shear the sheep."

So she pulls out her *Knit Your Way to Happiness* book and says, "Nope. Says right here you can dye the whole sheep." In fact, she already had another pan of bright pink "syrup" bubbling on the stove.

POOR Sock. I wanted to open the gate in the fence and set that sorry sheep free. But his own herd would probably turn against him, now that he's yellow as a dandelion. Kind of like how baby Mooshrooms turn against their mothers when their mushrooms get sheared off.

So Sock was probably feeling all weird and yellow and alone—just like me (I mean, except for the yellow part). And as we both stood there, wanting to jump the fence, I figured it out. I suddenly knew EXACTLY what Eddy meant about being "your own kind of creeper."

I mean, I hadn't turned myself yellow, but I'd pretty much turned myself into a whole different creeper trying to impress Connor. I stopped rapping in front of him. I put away my drawings. I pretended I didn't like Kid Z, for crying out loud! AND I started breaking the law.

Plus, I was mean to Sam, who—let's face it—is pretty much the best friend I've got at Mob Middle School. At least he used to be. So it's time for me to take a look at my 30-Day Plan. See, my old plan was all about getting a new best friend. But I sure don't want THAT anymore.

In fact, I really want my old friend back. I'm kind of missing the bouncy green dude. And he's a WAY better friend than Connor.

So my new plan goes something like this:

30 Days to a New Best Friend

~~Show Connor how awesome I am (easy, right?)~~
Show SAM I'm sorry.

~~Stick close to Connor at school (so he can SEE my awesomeness every second of every school night).~~
Stick close to Sam at school.

~~Give Sam some lessons in playing it cool (so the slime doesn't blow it for me)~~
Teach CONNOR a lesson about being too cool for school.

I could just let Connor off the hook—walk away and hope he leaves me alone. But he probably won't. I mean, he's got dirt on me, with that vending machine thing. And I don't want to spend my whole life watching over my shoulder for the C.I.A. (Creeper Intelligence Agency) to show up and pin that robbery on me.

So I have a plan for teaching Connor a lesson, but I'm going to need Sam's help. He might shoot me down. I might end up all yellow and alone in a field somewhere. (You know what I mean.)

But, hey, a creeper's gotta try.

DAY 24: SATURDAY

Sam ignored me at school last night. But that's okay.
See, I know where the slime lives.

So tonight, I walked through the swamp toward his
house. It's a long way there, and REALLY wet. But I
had a plan. And it had to do with a certain Cat Cam.

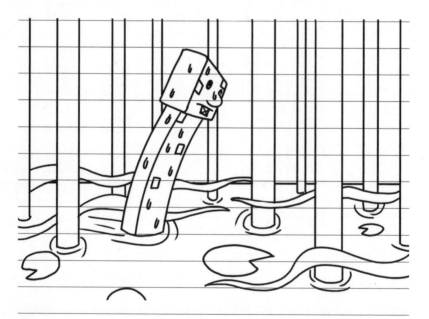

Sam was out back on his trampoline. It's this big
block of slime, and a slime bouncing on slime is a
really BOUNCY slime.

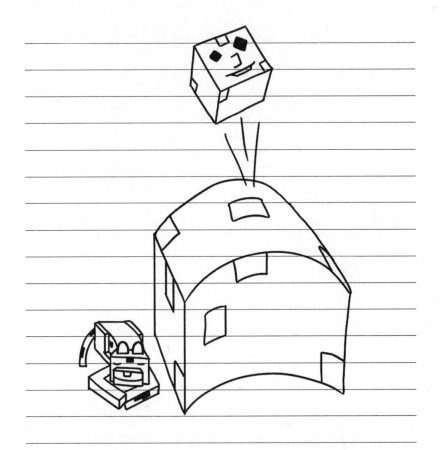

Sam was sky high, but Moo was sitting on the
ground. So I got as close to that cat as I could
without feeling like I was going to have a panic
attack. I actually sat down on the ground and looked
at her. And I started talking to her, all mushy like
the way Sam does.

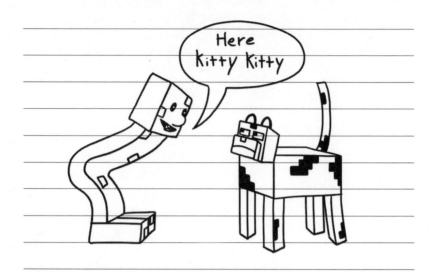

I wasn't trying to win over the cat. I was trying to win over SAM.

See, I know the way to Sam's heart. If I were trying to apologize to Ziggy Zombie, I'd serve him a rotten flesh sandwich. But with Sam, it's all about that cat. And it worked. Sort of.

Sam got off the trampoline as soon as he saw me, but he was still pretty wiggly and wobbly when he came over to see what I was doing.

"Hey! Why are you talking to Moo?" he wanted to know.

I shrugged. "I've kind of missed her," I fibbed.

"Really?" said Sam. My plan was already starting to work. That's what I like about Sam. He doesn't hold a grudge for very long.

I told him that I was actually hoping to see a couple of Cat Cam videos while I was over. Did he have any new ones?

Well, THAT did the trick. He bounced into the house and came out with his camera. And the video he showed me was actually REALLY funny.

See, Willow Witch had brewed a *potion of invisibility.*
And I guess Moo got into the potion. And turned
invisible. And when she started batting at Sam's
little brothers, the mini slimes, they didn't know
what was happening!

One of them got a paw across the face. Another
one got LICKED and started laughing hysterically.
And the whole time, those mini slimes were
bouncing around in circles trying to find Moo, the
Invisible Cat.

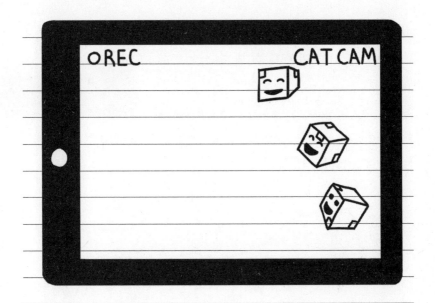

I laughed so hard my stomach hurt. So Sam played it again. And again.

By the time the battery in his camera died, it was like we were best buds again. But I knew I still had some apologizing to do.

So I put it to Sam straight. I said, "I'm sorry I didn't treat you very well when Connor was around. And I'm sorry about the rap songs—about writing them, and then about saying YOU wrote them. And I'm sorry about teasing you about Willow Witch. And about Moo. Oh, and about the mushroom stew."

Man, my apology list was sure long. I probably should have written it all down to make sure I didn't forget anything.

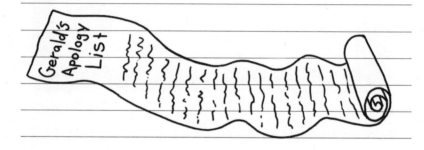

Gerald's Apology List

Sam nodded, his green head wiggling. And he kind of sniffled a little. But when he went in for a hug, I had to dodge it. I mean, that's where I draw the line. (Being hugged by a slime feels like drowning in a bowl of green Jell-o.)

Anyway, Sam and I were good after that. PHEW. But I still needed his help to teach Connor a lesson. And it was kind of a dangerous mission—the kind of mission you could really use a witch for, plus her potion of invisibility.

Sam said he'd talk to Willow. And with Willow Witch, things could go either way. See, unlike Sam, she DOES hold a grudge.

So now I'm just waiting. Which is like waiting for dye to dry or sheep's wool to grow.

Did I mention Sock is hot pink now?

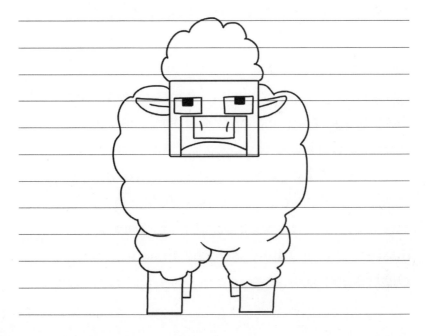

DAY 27: TUESDAY

So Sam told me at school last night that he and Willow are IN. I guess Willow Witch was kind of on to Connor all along. And she's ready to take that creeper down a notch.

We met after school this morning and talked it all through. Willow will bring her potion of invisibility. Sam will bring his Cat Cam. Oh, and his cat.

I've got the worst job. See, I have to find a way to bring CONNOR to the scene. And we're not exactly on speaking terms.

But I learned a thing or two from Connor while we were co-criminals. See, he's a prankster. And the best way to deal with a prankster is to prank him right back. I have to make him THINK we're doing one thing, and then do something completely different. Like he did with the fireworks on Mushroom Island.

So I wrote *him* a note and slid it onto his desk
during Language Arts. It said something like this:

I'm WAY low on
emeralds
Vending machine —
You and me —
Thursday morning
after school?

I didn't know if he would go for it. I really didn't. I
mean, he's a pretty smart creeper.

But I've figured out something else about Connor
Creeper. See, I think he's kind of lonely. Like Sock
the Sheep. Or like I was until Sam forgave me.

He studied my note for a while. And then, sure enough, he looked at me and nodded—that nod that says "We're ON."

So I guess we're doing this thing. And when it's all over, I'll have fixed the Connor problem. OR Mom will be dying Sock in black and white stripes so that she can knit me some sweaters to wear in prison.

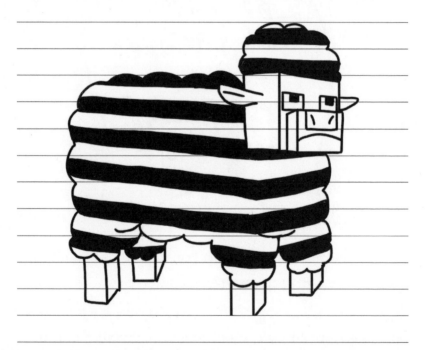

DAY 29: THURSDAY

My heart is still racing. SERIOUSLY. It's like I just ran a marathon.

Sam is here, too, and we've watched the whole prank back on Cat Cam. It looks something like this:

Connor showed up at the vending machine, right on time. But I wasn't there. At least he didn't KNOW I was there.

See, I'd taken a swig of invisibility potion. And so had Sam. And so had Willow. And so had Moo the Cat.

So Connor saw a note on the vending machine and read it. (I wrote that note, and I'm pretty proud of what I came up with.)

It said:

> Dear Connor,
> Sorry I had to bail.
> Bad stomach ache.
> I either ate too many pork chops
> while I was waiting for you,
> or Mad Mooshroom Disease strikes again.
> G.

He kind of chuckled when he read it, which was a good sign—that meant he bought my excuse. And then he got right to work, just like I knew he would. He pulled that key out of his backpack and opened up the front of the vending machine. And all those emeralds poured out into his sack.

Sam caught the whole thing on Cat Cam. Connor didn't even notice that camera floating in the air in the cafeteria. He was too busy stealing his loot.

But the best part came next. See, Moo has a thing for creepers. If she knows a creeper doesn't like her (and let's face it, most of us don't), she's ALL OVER that creeper. The more a creep dislikes her, the more she wants to love up on him. It's a cat thing.

And Connor REALLY dislikes cats. So right away, Moo must have been rubbing up against his legs, because he jumped sky high. Then she meowed, and he spun around searching for her. His eyes were HUGE, as if he'd seen the ghost of Herobrine himself.

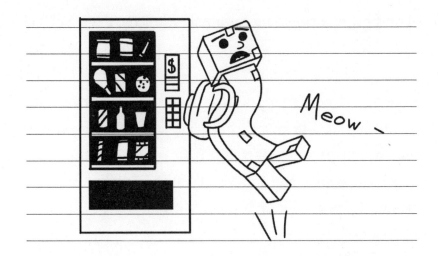

When the potion of invisibility wore off and Moo was suddenly standing RIGHT by Connor, he SCREAMED. Like a baby villager. And jumped up on the lunch table.

And did I mention Sam caught the whole thing on Cat Cam?

Course, I kind of forgot that if Moo wasn't invisible anymore, WE weren't either. And when Connor saw me, he was mad as a zombie pigman. He started hissing and shaking, and we all ran for cover—because I was sure that creeper was going to blow.

Well, he didn't. I guess he has SOME self-control. Instead, he told me that I was going DOWN. That he was going to tell the WHOLE school how I stole emeralds with him. How it was MY idea to bring fireworks to Mushroom Island.

That's when Sam waved the Cat Cam in the air and said he had Connor on video. Stealing emeralds. All by himself. Oh, and screaming like a baby villager at the sight of a cat.

Well, THAT shut Connor right up. I thought for a second he was going to charge Sam, but then he caught sight of Willow. She had a few bottles of potion in her hands, and by the look on her face, he could tell she wasn't afraid to use them.

"So here's how it's going to work, creep," I said, all gruff-like. (I'd been practicing that voice, just in case I DID end up I jail.) "You lay off me. You quit stealing emeralds. You give the zombie janitor back his key. You ditch the stash of fireworks you were planning to use to blow up the Strategic Exploding field. And you put the kibosh on any other criminal plan you've got in mind for Mob Middle School. If you DON'T, the video goes public. Got it?"

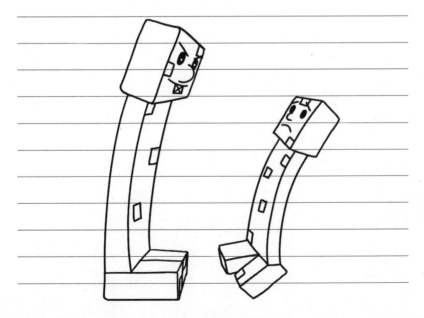

161

He stared at me hard. I like to think he was a LITTLE bit impressed. So maybe in the end, I DID show Connor Creeper how awesome I was. But I couldn't have done it without my friends.

Once he'd agreed to our arrangement, we went our separate ways, Connor Creeper and me. He slipped out the back door. And I went out the front door with Sam, Willow, and Moo.

I won't say that cat was growing on me. That would be a lie. But maybe I didn't mind her so much if she kept her distance.

And now we're all back at my house, where things are starting to feel normal again—I mean, except for the rainbow-colored sheep out back.

When Sam and Willow saw Sock, I just said, "Don't even ask."

But Mom and I are going to have to have a talk about that sheep—and this knitting thing. Once my heart stops pounding in my ears and I can breathe again.

DAY 30: FRIDAY

So Connor was _pretty quiet_ at school last night.

He was nice to Chloe when she started telling him about Strategic Exploding class. He sat by Ziggy Zombie at lunch, and from the next table over, I didn't hear him make a SINGLE comment about Ziggy's rotten flesh sandwich.

And when a witch asked if he could loan her an emerald for the vending machine, he said, "Sorry, but I'm fresh out of emeralds."

I knew THAT was true, because we'd made him put them all back into the machine yesterday morning.

So maybe there's hope for Connor yet. Or maybe he's just being nice because he thinks I have dirt on him. Between you and me, Sam and I got rid of that video right away. Having "dirt" on other mobs just makes me feel, well, dirty.

Connor can worry about that video all he wants, and he probably will. But no one's ever going to see him screaming like a baby villager over that cat. And he's not going to get locked up for emerald theft— at least not if he decides to creep a straight line from here on out.

So things are better now, but everything is NOT back to normal. I mean, there are still mobs at school that are mad at me about the whole rap song thing. So I'm still working on that.

Oh, and when I got home from school this morning, I saw that Sock the Sheep had made a new friend—a very NOT normal friend. Want to know who?

SIR COUGHS-A-LOT.

Yup, that old neighbor cat was rubbing up against Sock's legs like a baby Mooshroom loving up its momma.

At first, I was horrified. Then I saw that Sock was kind of enjoying the attention. At least he wasn't running away or trying to jump the fence anymore.

So I guess Sir Coughs-a-Lot doesn't mind that Sock is a multi-colored sheep. And I guess Sock doesn't mind that Sir Coughs-a-Lot is like NOT a sheep at all.

Maybe those two are like Sam and me. I'm not a slime, and he's not a creeper. But we get along pretty well. REALLY well actually. Every mob needs someone to hang out with, no matter what color you are or whether you have two legs or four.

So, I was heading for bed, because it's been a l-o-n-g 30 days. But then I heard Mom's knitting needles clacking away in the living room. And I decided it was time to stage an intervention. That's like when you get a bunch of people together, and you sit down someone you love and say THIS HAS GOT TO STOP. The knitting thing, I mean.

I found Dad in the garage, burning a few sweaters in the fire pit. So I knew he'd be on board with my plan.

And Cate's closet has been bulging with lumpy
sweaters and infinity scarves that everyone
knows she is NEVER going to wear. (She's way too
fashionable for that.)

So as soon as Chloe got home, all of us went into
the living room. Mom was like, "What's up?"

And everyone turned to ME to do the talking. Except
I hadn't really planned what I was going to say.

So I did what I sometimes do in uncomfortable
situations. I started to rap.

And when I finished my rap, Mom burst into tears.
And threw down her knitting needles.

"No!" she said. "I'm not happy. I HATE knitting."

Well, we all breathed a huge sigh of relief. I saw Dad kind of crawl up out of his turtleneck, like the coast was finally clear and he could come out now.

"So why are you DOING it?" asked Chloe. "If you don't like it, I mean."

Mom shrugged. "I don't know," she said. "Because Aunt Constance said I should. And she's so GOOD at it!"

I went all Eddy Enderman and said, "Mom, you gotta be your own creeper. Stay cool."

She looked at me like I was super wise. (I'll bet Eddy gets that a lot.)

But then I had a panicky thought. "Do we still get to keep Sock?" I asked. "Because, I mean, CAMMY is kind of attached to him." I didn't mention that the sheep was growing on me, too.

"Of course," said Mom. "In fact, I'm thinking that once I quit knitting, I might get some chickens."

Say WHAT?

Looks like Mom is off and running on a new plan. And I probably will be too one of these days.

But for now, I'm just going to focus on being my own kind of creeper. The kind that draws. And raps. And has Kid Z posters on his bedroom walls. Every. Single. One.

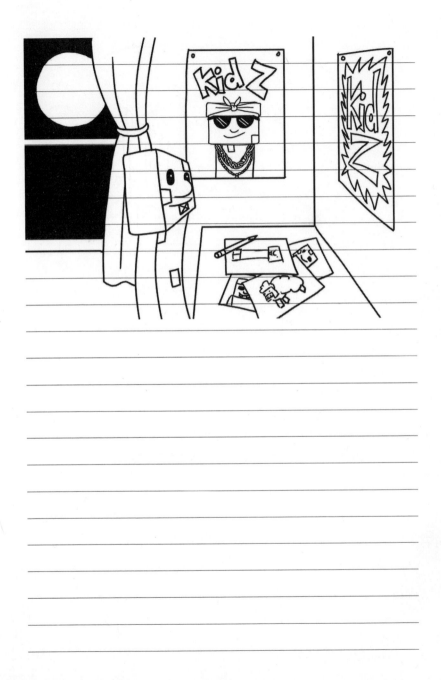